THIS WALKER BOOK BELONGS TO:

_____

_____

_____

For Rufus ♥

First published 2005 by Walker Books Ltd
87 Vauxhall Walk, London SE11 5HJ

This edition published 2006

2 4 6 8 10 9 7 5 3 1

© 2005 Lucy Cousins

The author/illustrator has asserted her moral rights

This book was handlettered by Lucy Cousins

Printed in China

British Library Cataloguing in Publication Data:
a catalogue record for this book is available from the British Library

ISBN-13: 978-1-4063-0156-4
ISBN-10: 1-4063-0156-6

www.walkerbooks.co.uk

Hooray for Fish!

Lucy Cousins

WALKER BOOKS
AND SUBSIDIARIES
LONDON · BOSTON · SYDNEY · AUCKLAND

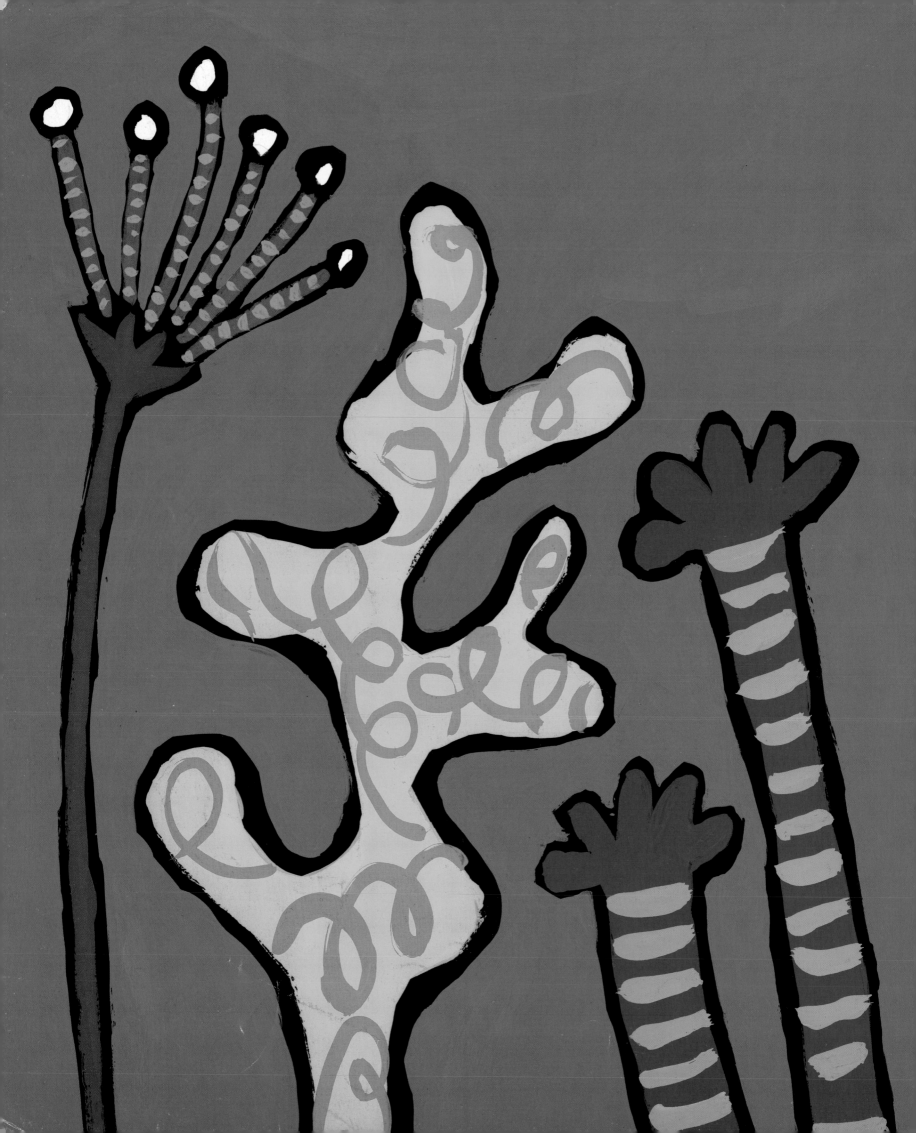

Hello! I am Little Fish,
swimming in the sea.
I have lots of fishy friends.
Come along with
me.

Hello, hello, hello, fish,

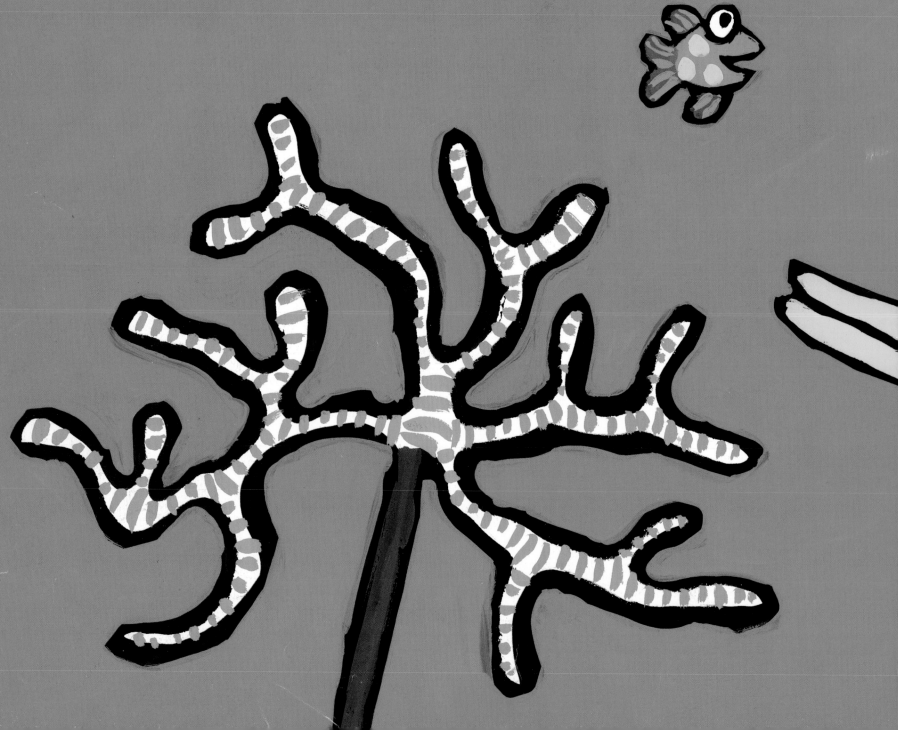

red,
blue

and yellow fish.

Hello, spotty fish,

stripy fish,

happy fish,

grumpy fish.

One,
two,
three...

2 2 2 2 2 2

3 3 3 3 3 3 3

How many can you see?

Hello, ele-fish,

shelly

fish.

Hello,
hairy fish,

scary fish,

eye fish,

shy
fish,

fly fish,

sky fish.

Hello,
fat and
thin fish.

Hello, twin

fin-fin fish.

Curly Whirly,

twisty twirly,

upside
down,

round and round.

So many friends,

So many **fish,**

splosh, splash, **splish!**

But where's the one
I love the best,
even more
than all the rest?

Hello, Mum.
Hello, Little Fish.

Kiss, kiss, kiss,
Hooray for fish!

WALKER BOOKS is the world's leading
independent publisher of children's books.
Working with the best authors and illustrators
we create books for all ages, from babies
to teenagers – books your child will
grow up with and always remember. So…

FOR THE BEST CHILDREN'S BOOKS,
LOOK FOR THE BEAR